Marianne Mitchell

JOE CINDERS

Illustrated by Bryan Langdo

Henry Holt and Company ★ New York

Henry Holt and Company, LLC
Publishers since 1866
115 West 18th Street
New York, New York 10011
www.henryholt.com

Henry Holt is a registered trademark of Henry Holt and Company, LLC
Text copyright © 2002 by Marianne Mitchell
Illustrations copyright © 2002 by Bryan Langdo
All rights reserved.
Distributed in Canada by H. B. Fenn and Company Ltd.

Library of Congress Cataloging-in-Publication Data
Mitchell, Marianne.
Joe Cinders / Marianne Mitchell; illustrations by Bryan Langdo.
Summary: With a "Hot diggety dog!" and a wave of his white sombrero, cowboy
Joe Cinders gets the girl in this Southwestern retelling of the Cinderella story.
[1. Fairy tales.] I. Langdo, Bryan, ill. II. Title.
PZ8.M68 Jo 2002 [E]—dc21 2001002669

ISBN 0-8050-6529-6 / First Edition—2002 / Designed by Martha Rago
The artist used Winsor & Newton watercolors on Aquarelle Arches paper
to create the illustrations for this book.
Printed in the United States of America on acid-free paper. ∞
3 5 7 9 10 8 6 4 2

* * *

To Cowboy Don and Cowgirl Pesha

—M. M.

For Mike, Scott, Bill, and George

—B. L.

* * *

Way out West, where dreams come true, lived a
poor cowboy named Joe Cinders. He had three lazy stepbrothers
who spent their days counting buzzards in the sky. Joe did all
the chores.

One day, a letter came.

"Hot diggety dog!" yelled Joe. "Miss Rosalinda's invited us to the fall fiesta at the Rancho Milagro."

"Lemme see that," said Butch. "Humph! This invite is for the Bronco boys. That's me, Buck, and Bart. Not you, ya little step-skunk!"

"Aw, gee," mumbled Joe. Too bad his ma and step-pa got swept away in a gully washer. Those Bronco boys had treated him like dirt ever since.

"Says here we're supposed to wear costumes to the party," said Butch. "How will pretty li'l Rosalinda know I'm the one she wants to dance with?"

"She won't care," crowed Buck, "'cause she'll be a-two-steppin' with me!"

"Mebbe so," said Bart. "But I'm the one who's gonna sashay Rosalinda up to the preacher. I hear tell she's scouting for a husband."

"She is?" asked Joe.

"Are you still here?" snarled Bart. "You've got chores to do. Now git!"

Joe plodded out to the barn. The thought of his grubby stepbrothers dancing with Rosalinda made his blood boil. He'd been sweet on her ever since the spring rodeo. But she was the richest rancher west of the Rio Grande, and he was just a poor cowboy.

Still, a guy could dream, couldn't he?

The Bronco boys argued all week about their costumes.

As usual, Joe fed the cows, baled the hay, and mended five miles of barbed-wire fences.

Not once did his stepbrothers do a lick of work.

Joe even had to tote all the hot water so they could take their once-a-year baths.

The day of the big fiesta, Butch decked himself out as a bank robber, Buck as a train robber, and Bart as a stagecoach robber. They gave their boots a lick and a polish and hopped in the buckboard.

"Now you take real good care of the herd while we're gone, little step-skunk," said Butch. "Don't you let one single dogie get away!" And with a crack of the reins they drove off in a cloud of dust.

That night, Joe Cinders sadly rode the range on his old horse. A lone coyote howled nearby. Suddenly a light shot across the sky and fell to earth. Joe peered into the darkness as sparks swirled like dust devils up ahead.

There stood a fella with baggy old overalls, a wool serape, and a crooked stick in his hand.

"Are you lost, mister?" asked Joe.

"Nope. I'm here to get you to that fiesta."

Joe slid off his horse. "Oh, sure. How can I go to a fancy dance in these raggedy clothes?"

"How about these?" The man waved his stick at Joe.

KA-ZOWIE!

Joe now wore brand-new jeans, a blue checkered shirt,
a white sombrero, and bright red boots.

"How'd you do that?" he gasped, admiring himself. "Aw, but I still can't go. My old horse would never get past the front gate."

"This will." The stranger waved his stick again.

A bright red pickup stood where Joe's horse had been.

"Wow," said Joe, running his hand along the shiny chrome bumper.

"But I'm supposed to watch the herd tonight. If I lose even one cow, I'll be in a heap of trouble."

"I'll fix that." The man waved his stick at a family of prairie dogs.

A dozen cowboys pranced about on their pinto ponies, ready to take over for Joe.

"Who are you?" Joe asked.

"Never you mind. Just get yourself over to that fiesta. But be careful! You have to leave when the fireworks start at midnight."

"Hot diggety dog!" cried Joe. He hopped into the red truck and zoomed across the desert to Rancho Milagro.

And not a second too soon! The prize bull had just busted out of the corral and was charging through the fiesta, breaking glasses and scattering people.

"Do something!" shrieked Rosalinda, shoving Butch, Buck, and Bart toward the bull.

"Oh, no!" said Butch. "Not me!"

"We're not that loco," said Buck and Bart.

Joe jumped out of his truck, pulled out his rope, and
snagged that bull before anyone could say "Howdy!"
"Bravo!" said Rosalinda.

From then on, no one else got a minute of Rosalinda's time. She and Joe whirled across the dance floor as the mariachi band played. Joe told her stories about life on the range. Rosalinda told him all about her plans for the ranch. The Bronco boys tried to cut in, but Joe wouldn't let them.

"No fair!" huffed Butch.

"Who is that guy?" asked Buck.

"Looks kinda familiar, don't he?" said Bart.

All too soon it was time for the fireworks show.

Whoosh! Boom! The night sky filled with glittering sparks.

Joe turned to Rosalinda and said, "Thank ya, ma'am, but I'd best be going now."

Whoosh! Boom! Bright colors lit up the dark.

"No, don't go!" cried Rosalinda.

Whoosh! Boom! Another rocket exploded in the air.

Joe raced for the gate. But his pickup truck had already turned back into his old horse. As Joe grabbed for the reins, he caught his boot in a prairie-dog hole.

"Forget the boot! I gotta get out of here!" he cried, and he galloped off to check on the herd.

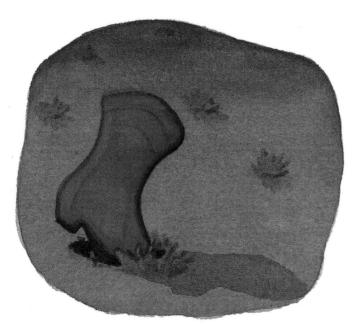

The next day as Joe did his chores, he thought only of
Rosalinda. He paid no attention to his stepbrothers' talk
about the mysterious stranger who had spoiled their fun at
the fiesta.

A few days later, Rosalinda arrived at the ranch. Joe was too busy busting a cantankerous pony to go meet her. As he jolted up and down, he saw Rosalinda chatting with the Bronco boys. She handed them a familiar red boot. First Butch tried getting it on, then Buck, then Bart.

"Stupid boot!" snarled Bart, hurling it way out into the corral. It hit Joe's pony.

"Yeeee-HA!" hollered Joe
as the pony reared up and
tossed him into the air.
When he came tumbling down,
his foot landed
          –PLOP!–
right in the
red boot
and . . .

KA-ZAM!

There he stood, dressed like he was at the fiesta.

"Well, I'll be!" said Rosalinda, running over to him.
"You'll be what?" asked Joe.
"Your ever-lovin' wife, if you want me."
Joe tossed his hat in the air. "Hot diggety dog!"

After a big wedding, Joe and Rosalinda turned her place into the Red Boot Dude Ranch. To show he had no hard feelings, Joe gave a job to each of his stepbrothers. Butch became the main stockholder. Buck managed the water resources. And Bart handled all the pressing problems of the ranch.

That left Joe and Rosalinda free to entertain their guests—
especially a certain mysterious fella with baggy old overalls,
a wool serape, and a crooked stick who had made their dreams
come true.